Learning to Read, Step by Step!

Ready to Read   Preschool–Kindergarten
• big type and easy words • rhyme and rhythm • picture clues
For children who know the alphabet and are eager to begin reading.

Reading with Help   Preschool–Grade 1
• basic vocabulary • short sentences • simple stories
For children who recognize familiar words and sound out new words with help.

Reading on Your Own   Grades 1–3
• engaging characters • easy-to-follow plots • popular topics
For children who are ready to read on their own.

Reading Paragraphs   Grades 2–3
• challenging vocabulary • short paragraphs • exciting stories
For newly independent readers who read simple sentences with confidence.

Ready for Chapters   Grades 2–4
• chapters • longer paragraphs • full-color art
For children who want to take the plunge into chapter books but still like colorful pictures.

STEP INTO READING® is designed to give every child a successful reading experience. The grade levels are only guides; children will progress through the steps at their own speed, developing confidence in their reading. The F&P Text Level on the back cover serves as another tool to help you choose the right book for your child.

Remember, a lifetime love of reading starts with a single step!

Visit us on the Web!
StepIntoReading.com
Seussville.com
pbskids.org/catinthehat
treehousetv.com

Educators and librarians, for a variety of teaching tools, visit us at
RHTeachersLibrarians.com

Library of Congress Cataloging-in-Publication Data
Rabe, Tish.
Now you see me / by Tish Rabe ; based on a television script by Katherine Standford ; illustrated by Christopher Moroney.
   p. cm. — (Step into reading. Step 2)
"Based in part on The Cat in the Hat Knows a Lot About That!"
ISBN 978-0-375-86706-4 (trade) — ISBN 978-0-375-96706-1 (lib. bdg.) — ISBN 978-0-449-81403-1 (ebook)
I. Stanford, Katherine. II. Moroney, Christopher, ill. III. Cat in the hat knows a lot about that! (Television Program). IV. Title.
PZ8.3.R1145Now 2011 [E] —dc22 2009051723

Printed in the United States of America
20 19 18 17 16 15

This book has been officially leveled by using the F&P Text Level Gradient™ Leveling System.

Now You See Me...

by Tish Rabe

based on a television script
by Katherine Standford

illustrated by Christopher Moroney

Random House 🏠 New York

Nick said, "It's vacation!
And we have all week
to play games and have fun.
Want to play hide-and-seek?"

"You count and I'll hide,"
Sally said. "And you'll see—
I'll hide so well that
you'll never find me!"

Sally looked till she found
a good hiding spot.
". . . Ten!" Nick called out.
"Coming! Ready or not!"

Where was Sally hiding?
In less than a minute,
Nick ran to the wheelbarrow
and found Sally in it!

"Hide-and-seek!" cried the Cat.

"Oh, I'm so glad I came!

The counting! The hiding!

It's my favorite game!"

"It's great!" Nick agreed.

Sally said as she sighed,

"But Nick always finds me

wherever I hide."

"Aha!" said the Cat.
"We must leave right away
to meet my friend Gecko,
who plays every day.

He hides in the day
and also at night.
It helps him stay safe
to keep out of sight."

So they flew to the jungle.

It was steamy and hot.

"My friend," said the Cat,

"is not easy to spot.

Cam-ou-flage helps him hide.

It is his hiding trick."

"Cam-ou-*what*? I don't know

what that word means!" said Nick.

"I'll explain," said the Cat. "Camouflage is the way some animals stay out of sight every day.

Camouflage helps them hide

so they will not be found.

It helps them blend in

with whatever's around."

"That Gecko blends in.
He's not easy to see."
"Hello!" Gecko called.
"Are you looking for me?
My tail looks leaf-like
and my skin is light brown.
I'm hanging right here in
this tree upside down!"

"Could you show us," asked Sally,
"how to hide like you do?
We want to learn how
to use camouflage too!"
"In the jungle," said Gecko,
"your clothes are too bright.
You need to blend in
so you stay out of sight."

"We can't hide dressed like this,"
said Nick. "What to do?"
"You need help," said the Cat,
"from Thing One and Thing Two!"
"Can you help us," asked Sally,
"look leafy and green?
If we look like the jungle,
we'll never be seen."

So, before the kids knew it,
they got a surprise—
Things One and Two made
them the perfect disguise!

"Mr. Gecko," said Nick,

"you can hide, it is true.

But can you find us

when we're hiding from *you*?"

"Of course!" Gecko said,
but when he looked around,
those camouflaged kids
were nowhere to be found!

He looked in the shadows
and looked in the light.
They were hiding so well
they were nowhere in sight.

Then all of a sudden
a tree started to wiggle.
"Wait!" Gecko said.
"I just heard someone giggle!
Out here in the jungle,"
he said with a smile,
"the trees haven't giggled
in quite a long while."

"Nick," Sally asked,

"when I was hiding today,

how did you find where

I was right away?"

"Well," Nick said, "finding

you wasn't hard.

Your dress was the only pink

thing in my yard."

"Hide-and-seek," said the Cat,
"is so much fun to play.
I could play it with Gecko
and you every day.

But we have to go now.

We'll be back soon, I know.

Goodbye, Gecko!

Oh . . . Gecko?"

"NOW where did he go?"